To: Our three Precious
Angels - Bri -
Rae -
Megan

Grandpa +
Grandma Asman

Christmas CLASSICS for Children

Publishing House
St. Louis

CONTENTS

CHRISTMAS CLASSICS FOR CHILDREN

Copyright © 1981
Concordia Publishing House
3558 South Jefferson
Saint Louis, Missouri 63118

From
THE CITY THAT FORGOT ABOUT CHRISTMAS   Concordia Publishing House © 1968
JOURNEYS TO BETHLEHEM   Concordia Publishing House © 1974
LITTLE TREE AND HIS WISH   Concordia Publishing House © 1966
THE MYSTERIOUS STAR   Concordia Publishing House © 1974
THE STORY OF SILENT NIGHT   Concordia Publishing House © 1965

Manufactured in the United States of America

4 5 6 7 8 9 10 11 12 DB 92 91 90 89 88 87 86 85

Library of Congress Cataloging in Publication Data

Christmas classics for children.

Contents: The city that forgot about Christmas /
written by Mary Warren—Journeys to Bethlehem / retold
by Dorothy Van Woerkom—Little Tree and his wish /
written by Viola Rutz—[etc.]
     1. Christmas stories. 2. Children's stories, America
[1. Christmas stories]
PZ5.C4676   [Fic]   81-3270
ISBN 0-570-04058-2 (pbk.)   AACR2

THE CITY THAT FORGOT ABOUT CHRISTMAS

Written by Mary Warren
Illustrated by Rudolph Wendelin

There once was a city that had forgotten about God. The people were selfish and mean. The healthy people did not take care of the sick. The sick people complained. The hungry stole food.

The children fought. The grown-ups scowled and shouted. Nobody smiled any more. Worst of all, because the people in this city had forgotten the meaning of love, they had also forgotten the meaning of Christmas.

Christmas Day was like any ordinary day. Nobody sang the joyous Christmas songs. No mothers cooked a special Christmas dinner. No fathers helped their children trim a Christmas tree. There were no mysterious packages, no stockings hung by the fireside.

Can you imagine that? NO CHRISTMAS!

One day a stranger from a far country came to town. He was an old man named Matthew.

"What?" he cried when he discovered that nobody knew about Christmas. "Not one of you remembers the message of the angels? Well, we shall see what we shall see."

Matthew was a kind old man, and merry. In his younger days he had been a carpenter. He knew how to make many things out of scraps of wood. He could carve too.

He could make tops and whistles, dolls and jumping jacks with his pocketknife. Children trailed after him, wondering what he would make for them next.

Wives, when they heard his gay whistle, called to each other: "Here comes Matthew. Perhaps he will mend my doorstep." "When Matthew comes, I shall ask him to make me a new window box for my pansies."

The men liked to have him around too. He hiked out into the hills with them and showed them the best places to fish. Since he was retired and did not have to work anymore, he had time to help them with their jobs.

"The city is a different place since old Matthew came," said a mother.

"Yes," agreed her husband. "People are smiling again and doing things for one another. It seems to me there are fewer ugly words too."

Old Matthew was saddened by the thought that nobody could remember the Christmas story.

Late in the year when snow fell and the winds blew, he sat near his kitchen stove and began to carve something new.

"What is it?" asked the children. "Tell us, what are you making now?"

While he carved, Matthew began to tell the Christmas story. He told of the angel who appeared to Mary, and how Mary went to the hill country to carry the good news to her cousin Elizabeth.

"This is the angel," he told the children when he had finished his carving. Sure enough, the wooden figure was a life-sized angel.

The children looked at the angel and touched it and loved it.

"But what is the piece you are working on now?" they cried excitedly.

"It will be Mary," said Matthew. He pointed to a large piece of wood leaning against the wall. "And that will be Joseph."

"Hurry," begged the children. "Hurry so they will be finished in time for Christmas."

Old Matthew had told them so much about the Christmas season that all families in town decided to celebrate it this year. For the first time in anybody's memory, the city would have Christmas.

Everyone was humming and whistling and singing the carols Matthew had taught them. Mothers were stirring up puddings and baking cookies. Fathers were saying, "Come, children, we'll go out into the woods and cut the most beautiful tree we can find." Children were busy making colored paper chains and foil stars to hang on their trees.

17

People were hiding marvelous Christmas packages. Everybody was happy because Christmas was in the air.

"My father might like to help finish the figures for the Christmas creche," suggested one boy a week before Christmas. "He knows how to carve."

"Mine does too," chimed in another child.

"And," said a third, "my mother knows how to paint. I'm sure she would like to help."

Matthew smiled, and the smile on his wrinkled face was wonderful to see. "You may *all* help," he said. "Tell your families to come to my house tonight, and I will show them what to do."

Every night after that, mothers and fathers and children gathered around Matthew's kitchen stove and carved and painted and listened to his wonderful tales of Christmas.

Before many days passed, the statues of Joseph and Mary, the angel Gabriel, the shepherds, a donkey and some sheep and cows were completed.

"Before next Christmas we shall build a church," said a father one evening. "But this year, where will we set the creche?"

"My tool shop is heated," said another man. "We can clean it and use it for the stable."

"We still have the baby Jesus to carve," said a little girl.

"He will be in the creche by Christmas," promised Matthew.

Christmas Eve was one night away. Long after the people
had gone home to bed, Matthew sat up and put the finishing
touches on the statues.

The next morning he got up early and left the city. All day
long people wondered about him and looked for him. They were
busy cleaning the shop, making it into a stable with fresh, sweet
hay and setting the figures there. Before they knew it, evening
had come, but Matthew was not to be found.

The whole city was astir. "Perhaps he was called away or had an errand to do," the people told one other. "But surely he will come back before morning and bring the baby for the manger."

Seven o'clock. No Matthew!

Eight o'clock. No Matthew!

Nine o'clock. "How can we take our children to say a prayer at the stable when there is no baby?" asked a mother. Sadly, she wiped her eyes.

"Hush now," said another mother. "I have an idea." She whispered something in her husband's ear and he exclaimed, "Yes! I will tell the people that the stable is ready." Off he went.

When the people of the city came to the stable, the light was shining inside, and it was warm and smelled of fresh hay.

There in the crib was a baby sleeping peacefully under his soft blanket!

"Someone has put her own baby into the crib!" cried a child.

"A real live baby!" said the people as they knelt to pray.

"That is the message old Matthew was trying to bring us these many weeks," said the father of the baby. "On the first Christmas, God came to earth as a *real live baby*. Remember how Matthew always said: 'The Word was made flesh and dwelt among us. . .'?"

A murmur arose among the people as they said to one another, "It is a holy night. He is with us again!" And before leaving the stable, a child leaned down to kiss the baby lying in the manger, and she whispered softly, "He is with us again. God has come to our city. And do you suppose that Matthew might have been the angel who brought the message?"

Journeys to Bethlehem
the story of the first Christmas

Retold by Dorothy Van Woerkom
Art by Dhimitri Zonia

Moonlight flashed against the Roman soldier's helmet as he urged his horse up the narrow trail. Near the top of the hill, among the shadows of tall cypress, he could see the square white houses.

So this was Nazareth! The soldier was impatient and tired. Twice he had lost his way to this nuisance of a place. Well, no matter that it was late and the people were asleep—was he to wait in the hills until cock-crow? No! He would waken them.

"Arise!" he shouted above the clatter of his horse's hooves, above the cackle of startled chickens, above the bleat of frightened lambs. "Arise and listen, in the name of Caesar!"

In fear and amazement the people hurried to the market place. There, by torchlight, the soldier read the decree from Caesar Augustus that they should all be counted and taxed. "Each must go to his own city," the soldier said. "Each to the city of his fathers. Make haste, Nazarenes, to obey the command of the Emperor!"

He gave them neither smile nor nod but rolled up his scroll and spurred his horse to a gallop down the road.

The soldier was gone. The farm animals grew quiet again. But the people of Nazareth stared at each other in alarm. Most of them would have to leave their homes at once. Joseph, who was of the family of David, and Mary, his wife, must make the long journey to Bethlehem. And Mary's child would soon be born!

Joseph walked slowly back to his house.

But Mary was already preparing for the journey. She
had set out some round cheeses and small loaves of bread.
From the wall she took down the goatskins which they would
fill with water from the well in the morning. She saw how
sad Joseph looked.

"Do not fear for me," she told him.

"Then try to sleep," he said. "It is a while yet to sunrise."

So Mary returned to her pallet, while Joseph stood at the open doorway, praying in the moonlight.

They left Nazareth at dawn, Mary riding on the donkey and Joseph leading it gently down the hillside. The trail twisted and turned through the mountains and olive groves of Galilee, until at last it joined the hilly caravan road high above the Jordan River.

There were many people on the road, all going to be counted. Some hurried quickly by, with sandals flapping and walking sticks sharply tapping the hard dirt. Some plodded wearily behind oxcarts loaded with all their possessions. Others drove their sheep and goats ahead of them, having no one left at home to care for them.

Towards evening of the fourth day, Joseph suddenly stopped and pointed. On a distant hill was Bethlehem.

It was late when they entered the busy, noisy town. Wagons and carts crowded the narrow street. Camels and donkeys pawed the ground. People knocked at shop doors to bargain with the merchants for a room, because the inn was full.

"The inn is full! No room, no room!" Joseph, pushing his way into the courtyard, dragging the donkey, heard the innkeeper shout it. Still he pushed on, shouldering his way through the crowd.

He pounded on the door. No answer. He pounded harder. His great, calloused, carpenter's hands shook the heavy door on its pivots. The upper half swung open.

"Well?" demanded the innkeeper. "Did I not just say there is no room? Have you left your ears behind you in the country?"

Then he hesitated. Joseph's eyes were burning into his. Mary, pale and tired on the weary little donkey, made him suddenly anxious to help. Gently he said, "Go around to the back. There you will find a cave. It is a stable, but you will not do better anywhere in Bethlehem tonight."

The air had turned cool after sunset. Now it was bitter cold. How much warmer the cave was than the courtyard! Mary smiled up at Joseph.

"We will be safe here," she said. "The Babe will be safe here."

Joseph was looking around the cave. "See the manger," he said. "It has a crooked leg, but I can fix that. It will make a comfortable bed for the Child."

Two sleepy oxen and a donkey drew nearer to watch while Joseph mended the manger and Mary smoothed out the hay for a bed.

At midnight, Jesus was born. Mary wrapped Him in a long linen cloth, and Joseph laid Him gently in the manger. Together they cared for Him and watched over Him through the night.

In the hills not far from Bethlehem, shepherds huddled around a small fire. Thousands of stars filled the clear night sky. Now and then a shepherd yawned or spoke softly to another. Here and there on the hillside a lamb called out to its mother. And over all came the sad sweet music of the flute played by a shepherd sitting apart from the others on a rock.

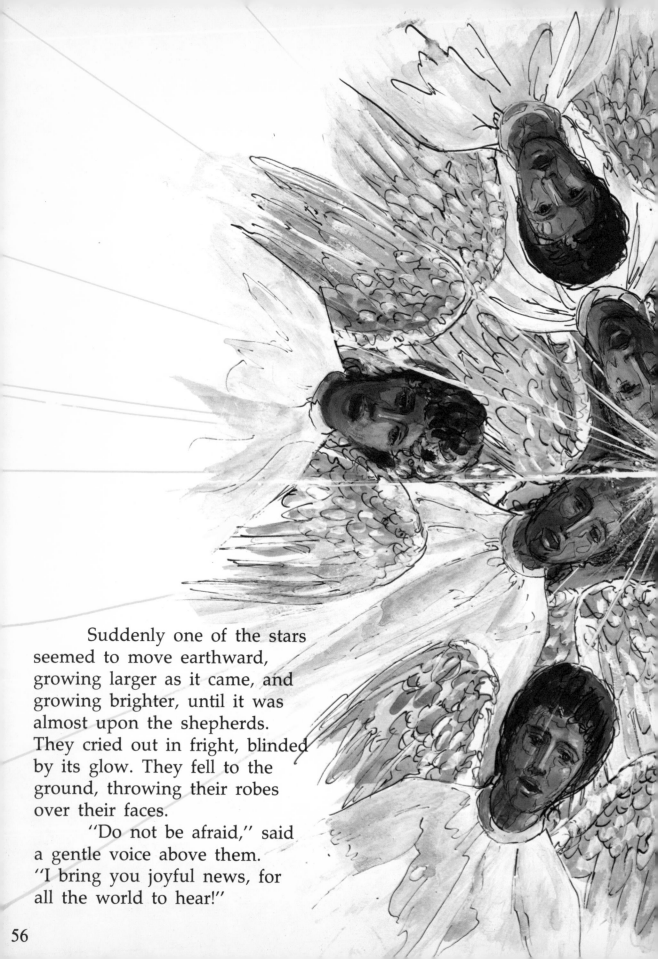

Suddenly one of the stars
seemed to move earthward,
growing larger as it came, and
growing brighter, until it was
almost upon the shepherds.
They cried out in fright, blinded
by its glow. They fell to the
ground, throwing their robes
over their faces.

"Do not be afraid," said
a gentle voice above them.
"I bring you joyful news, for
all the world to hear!"

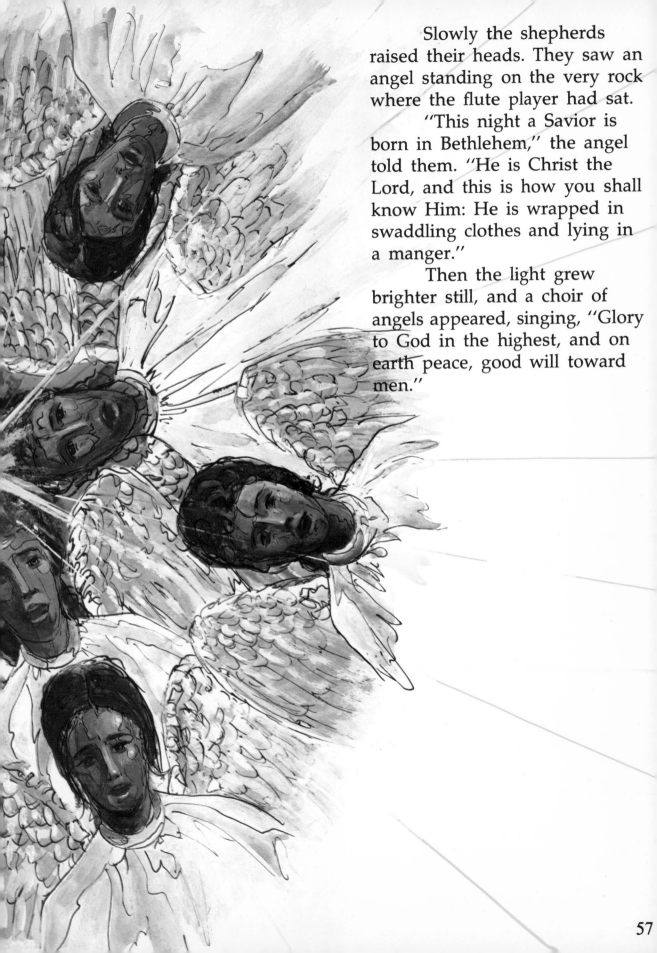

Slowly the shepherds raised their heads. They saw an angel standing on the very rock where the flute player had sat.

"This night a Savior is born in Bethlehem," the angel told them. "He is Christ the Lord, and this is how you shall know Him: He is wrapped in swaddling clothes and lying in a manger."

Then the light grew brighter still, and a choir of angels appeared, singing, "Glory to God in the highest, and on earth peace, good will toward men."

The angels disappeared with the last soft notes of their song, and the strange light faded. Once more the sky was clear and still. Yet the shepherds knelt in silence, until one of them cried,

"Let us go to Bethlehem and see this marvelous thing!"

So they drew lots for someone to stay behind with the sheep. The others hurried down to the town to find the Child in the manger. And, when they had found Him, they stopped all who would listen, to tell them the news of the Holy Child and what the angels had said of Him.

Now on the same midnight that Jesus was born, three Wise Men, who lived in a country far to the east, were watching the sky. They saw two strange stars moving toward each other. At last, on the eastern rim of the horizon, the stars came together. They formed a great ball of light, sweeping upwards across the sky, then moving slowly westward.

One of the Wise Men remembered that the Jews
believed a king would soon be born to them. Perhaps this
new star was the sign of his coming. They would go and see.
The way was long. They traveled by night, for they
could not see the star by day. Yet each evening at twilight
it appeared, leading them through hill and desert, through
rain and moonlight, through stillness and wind.

In Judea they stopped at Jerusalem, which they knew was the Holy City of the Jews. Certainly this was where their King would be born!

"Where is He that is born King of the Jews?" they asked again and again. "For we have seen His star in the East and have come to worship Him."

No one in Jerusalem had heard of such a King; but the cruel and wicked King Herod soon enough heard of the Wise Men! Herod stamped about his palace in a rage. Who was this, come to take his place? Who dared to call Himself King of the Jews?

Then Herod, also, remembered the Jewish prophecy about a king. He sent for his chief advisors.

"Tell me," he demanded, "where this King of Israel will be born."

They answered, "The Scriptures say in Bethlehem of Judea."

So Herod sent for the Wise Men and questioned them. They told him about the wonderful star and about the Child they sought.

"Then look in Bethlehem," Herod said, "and when you find Him, come and tell me, so that I may worship Him also."

But that night, while the Wise Men followed the star to Bethlehem, Herod plotted to kill the Child when they found Him.

The star did not lead to a palace as the Wise Men expected, but when they saw Jesus, they knew He was the King they had come to see. Bowing before Him, they offered their gifts of gold and frankincense and myrrh.

And when it came time to leave, an angel warned them in a dream that they should not return to Herod. They obeyed, going home by another way.

Then the angel came to Joseph. "Rise!" he said. "Herod's soldiers come to kill the Child. Flee from here at once! Take the Child and His mother to Egypt."

Joseph awoke at once. He saddled the donkey while Mary packed the saddlebags. They were on their way before daybreak. Hurrying across the hills and plains and desert, they traveled by night, rested by day, until at last they reached the safety of Egypt.

Time passed, and yet more time, until the angel came again, to tell Joseph of Herod's death.

King Herod was gone! Now they could return to Bethlehem! But when they came near Judea, they heard that Herod's son was king.

The son was as cruel as the father, and Joseph was afraid to remain in that country. He decided, instead, to follow the ancient road across the Plains of Sharon, northward into Galilee. He was bringing Mary and her Child to Nazareth—that little town so hidden in the hills that the Roman soldier nearly did not find it.

That what was spoken by the prophets might be fulfilled: "He shall be called a Nazarene."

Matthew 2:23 RSV

Little Tree and His Wish

Written by Viola Rutz

Illustrated by Jim Roberts

Many, many years ago in a forest across the sea,
there stood a very sad little tree.
He was a sad little tree, but he was not a lonely tree.
The animals of the forest loved him and came to
rest and play in his branches.

"Why are you sad, little friend?" asked the squirrels.
The little tree stood with drooping branches and answered,
"Nobody wants me. I'm scrawny and little and
my wood is not very good."

The sparrows twittering in the branches heard this
and scolded Little Tree.

"We don't think you are scrawny."

"We like to build nests in your branches."

"Please don't be sad, Little Tree."

"Thank you, my dear friends," answered Little Tree.

"I would indeed be a lonely tree without you to keep
me company."

Just then they heard footsteps on the forest floor.
"Sh-sh," said Little Tree, "here they come again."

A hushed stillness came over him.
The animals watched Little Tree trying to raise his
drooping branches.

"Why," whispered the chipmunk, "is Little Tree trying
to stand so straight and tall?"

The voices came closer.

Then they could see the woodsmen with their shiny axes.

The men stopped at a nearby tree.

"Here's a splendid tree," said a man.

"His wood will make a sturdy wall."

Little Tree and his friends watched the men while they chopped down the tree.

Finally the men went away.

Little Tree's branches slowly started to droop again.

"We like your branches better this way," chirped the birds.

"I wish I were a strong tree too," cried Little Tree.

"I wish someone would say that I'd make a sturdy wall."

The squirrels chattered among themselves, "Little Tree is strong. We like to hop and climb on him."

They said to Little Tree, "Please don't wish to go away, little friend."

"I just can't help it," sighed Little Tree.

"Just think of all the wonderful things these big strong trees can be."

"They can be houses or tables, boats or palaces."

"Imagine," said Little Tree dreamily, "the very best tree could even be a throne for a king!"

As the days went by Little Tree forgot the woodsmen
and began to be cheerful again.
The animals scampered and scurried back and forth
through him.
One hot afternoon he gave shade to some tired,
laughing children.

But then — the sound of the axe was again heard
in the forest.

The animals hoped Little Tree wouldn't be sad again.
Soon his branches were drooping more than usual.
The news went whispering through the forest,
"They are cutting the great-grandfather tree."
"The great-grandfather tree . . ."
"The great-grandfather tree . . ."
"He will be a large house for many people," said
the squirrels.

"Men will build him into a ship to sail far away,"
said the birds.

"Oh," sobbed Little Tree, "I wish somebody
wanted me!"

One day a little old man came into the forest.
He looked at the trees...

   the tall trees

    the short trees

     the old trees

      the young trees.

He stopped and looked at Little Tree.
The animals held their breath.
Little Tree looked as proud as he could.

"Yes, yes," the little old man said, "this is the tree
I want. This wood will be all right."

Little Tree cried to his friends, "Did you hear that?
He wants me! He wants me!"
The axe hit its first blow.
The animals said good-bye to the tree and flitted away.
Little Tree was so happy he hardly noticed the blows.
    "I wonder what I will be? A table? A chair?
A treasure chest?" wondered Little Tree.

Little Tree was excited and happy.
He kept guessing what he would be all the way to
the little old man's house.

When the little old man came to his house, he
took Little Tree out to the stable.
He dropped Little Tree in a corner.
Little Tree fell in the dark corner and stayed
there for a long, long time.

At first Little Tree was sad and lonely.
He was worried.
   "What will happen to me?" he asked.
   "Did he forget me?"
He missed his friends in the forest.
   "I wonder how they are?" he thought.

But then he started to watch the cows and the sheep.
   "The barn is a nice, cozy place," he said to himself.
He soon found new friends in all the animals in the barn.

One day the little old man came right to the dark corner.

"I knew you'd come in handy some time," said the little
old man as he picked up the little tree.

Then the little old man began to use his tools.

Little Tree was excited.

"What will I be? What will I be?" he said over and over
to himself.

"Yes, sir," the little old man said, "you were mighty
scrawny, but your wood will be all right for a manger."

"We need a sturdy manger to hold the hay for the cows."
Little Tree decided, "I'd rather be a manger than lonely
old wood in the corner."

"But how I dreamed of palaces and kings!"

For many years Little Tree held the sweet, moist hay
for the cattle.
He liked the low moo of the cows and the swish-swish of
their tails.

One night as the little old man came to the door of the stable
a man and a woman came to him. They looked tired.
Their clothes and feet were dusty, as if they had come
a long way.

"Good evening, Sir," they said.

"We are strangers here," explained the man.

"No one seems to have any room for us, and we are
waiting for our baby to arrive soon. My name is Joseph, and
this is my wife, Mary. Could we perhaps stay in the stable for
the night?"

"I'll be glad to help you out," said the little old man.

"There's plenty of hay to keep you warm and cozy."
And the little old man let them in.

Little Tree was all excited by the visit.
He thought, "And we'll soon have a baby here, too!"
Joseph made a bed of hay for Mary and himself in the corner,
and they lay down to rest.

After a while Joseph got up, looked around, and took the manger
to Mary's side.
They put fresh, clean hay into the manger.

It was then that Mary laid a beautiful baby boy
into the manger.
Little Tree's heart skipped a beat.
He never dreamed he'd cradle a sweet child!
Little Tree was so happy, "I like being a bed for a baby.
"The child is so warm and soft lying in the hay."

Then Little Tree heard many soft footsteps coming.

He looked and saw shepherds in the stable.

The shepherds told Mary and Joseph, "An angel told us the baby was born."

They said, "The whole sky was filled with angels singing praises to God."

The shepherds came closer to the manger.

They looked at the baby.

Little Tree could see how happy they were.

Quietly the shepherds kneeled.

Little Tree heard the shepherds pray:

"Thank you, dear Lord, for sending us Your Son!"

"Why," said Little Tree, "this child isn't just a sweet baby!

"This is a very special baby.

"This baby is God's Son!

"This baby is a King!"

And Little Tree thanked God that he could be a throne for such a very great King:

"Thank you, Dear God, for making me a scrawny little tree," he said.

"Why, had I been a big and beautiful tree, I would never be the manger now!"

THE MYSTERIOUS STAR

written by
Joanne Marxhausen

art by
Susan Stoehr Morris

To Jesus, the bright Morning Star

Jamie's father was reading him a story. "Long, long ago," his father read, "some men from a faraway country saw a new star in the sky. What a big star it was! So brightly it shone, and so beautiful! They followed the bright star. It led them to a little town called Bethlehem where they found the baby Jesus. He was the Savior and brought great joy and happiness to their lives."

"Oh, Daddy," said Jamie, "I want to see the star! Can I see the star too?"

He jumped off his father's lap and ran to the window. The night was dark and clear. The sky was dotted with millions of twinkling specks, but none of them seemed very important or more special than any other.

Jamie's father said, "If you keep looking, Jamie, you'll find the star, but not in the sky."

Jamie didn't understand what his father meant, but his mother said it was bedtime, and so he decided to think about it some more tomorrow.

Next morning after Jamie pulled on his trousers and his green-striped shirt, he ran to his mother and asked, "May I go for a walk? I'm going to look for the bright star!"

"Yes," said his mother and she smiled.

Jamie decided it might be a long walk, and he might get thirsty, so he asked his mother for a thermos of water to take along. Then he thought about how lonesome he might get if it took a long, long time to find the star, so he took his teddy bear along too. His mother packed him a peanut-butter-and-jelly sandwich in a paper bag just in case he got hungry on the way.

At last Jamie put the thermos of water, his teddy bear, and the peanut-butter-and-jelly sandwich into his red wagon and started off.

For a moment he wondered where he should look for the star. Then he thought about the church. He had heard many stories about Jesus there, and he thought he might see the star there too. So he walked to the church. But the windows were dark, and the door was closed. Jamie didn't see the star there.

Next he decided to walk to the park. On the way he saw a little girl who was crying.

"Nobody likes me," sobbed the little girl.

Jamie felt so sorry for her that a big tear rolled down *his* cheek.

"I like you," Jamie told the little girl, "and I know Some-one else who does. My best friend is Jesus. He likes you. He likes everybody!"

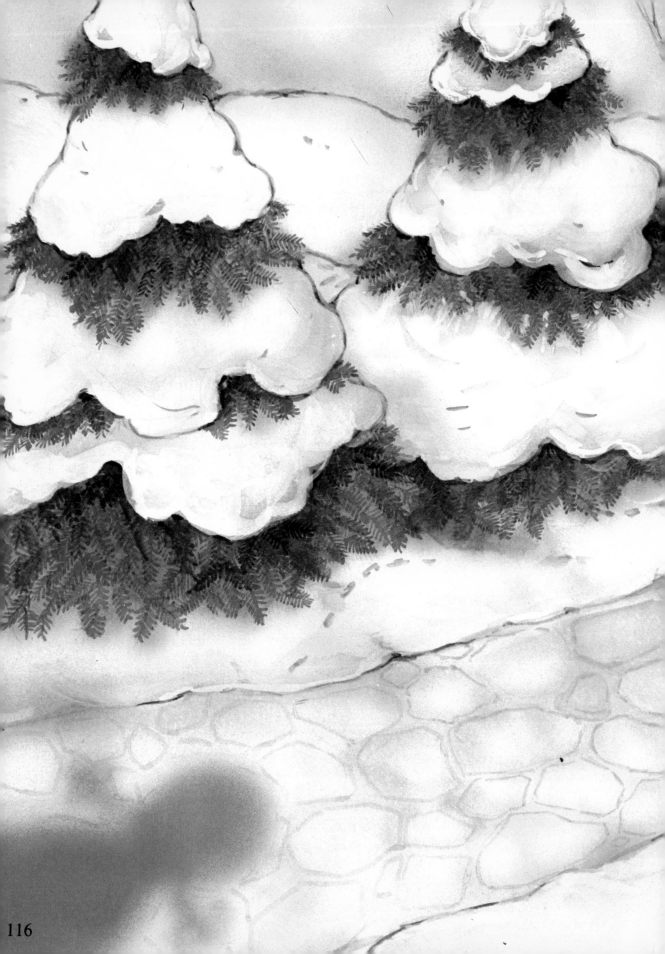

Then Jamie told her about the bright and beautiful star he was looking for and hurried off to look for it some more. He didn't notice he was being followed.

In the park Jamie saw an old man sitting all alone on a bench. He looked lonely, so Jamie climbed up beside him. He thought maybe the old man had seen the star since he lived long, long ago. So Jamie told him about the story.

"I've seen lots of things in my day," the old man said, "but I've never seen a star like that."

Then Jamie felt hungry. He wondered if the old man might like some of his peanut-butter-and-jelly sandwich.

"Sure would!" said the old man. "I haven't tasted a peanut-butter-and-jelly sandwich since I was a little boy."

"Tell me about when you were a boy," said Jamie. He listened and listened while the old man talked.

The old man didn't look so lonely anymore when Jamie climbed down off the park bench and started on his way again. Jamie walked and walked. He didn't notice he was being followed.

Then Jamie stopped by a big tree. It was all hung with frost and looked just like Christmas. It made Jamie feel good inside to think how God made such beautiful things. It made him feel like Christmas and singing. So he made up a song about how thankful he was that God makes beautiful things and as he walked along he sang the song. He walked past a little girl sitting on a stump. She didn't say anything, she just smiled.

So Jamie walked on, singing his song. He still didn't notice he was being followed.

Soon he came to a street corner where he saw a boy sitting beside a stack of newspapers. Jamie could tell the boy was very poor by the ragged clothes he was wearing. He looked tired too. Jamie told the boy all about the star he was looking for.

"I don't have time to look for a star," said the boy. "I have to earn all the money I can delivering newspapers."

Jamie wondered if a drink of water might make the boy feel better. He got the thermos of water out of his wagon and offered it to the boy. The boy took a big drink.

"Oh, thank you!" he said. "Now I feel good enough to deliver the rest of these papers."

128

Jamie walked on and on. He walked past the toy store, but there was no bright and beautiful star there. He saw lots of goodies in the candy shop, but he didn't see a bright and shining star. How happy he would be if only he could find it! He searched and searched, but no star did he see. He still didn't notice he was being followed.

Up ahead Jamie saw a little boy on roller skates. He'd fallen down. Jamie ran to see if the boy was hurt. Sure enough! He was crying. He had bumped his knee. Jamie remembered

how his mother kissed his hurts sometimes and made them feel better. He kissed the little boy's knee. The little boy was so surprised, he forgot how his knee hurt. He stopped crying and listened while Jamie told him the story about the star.

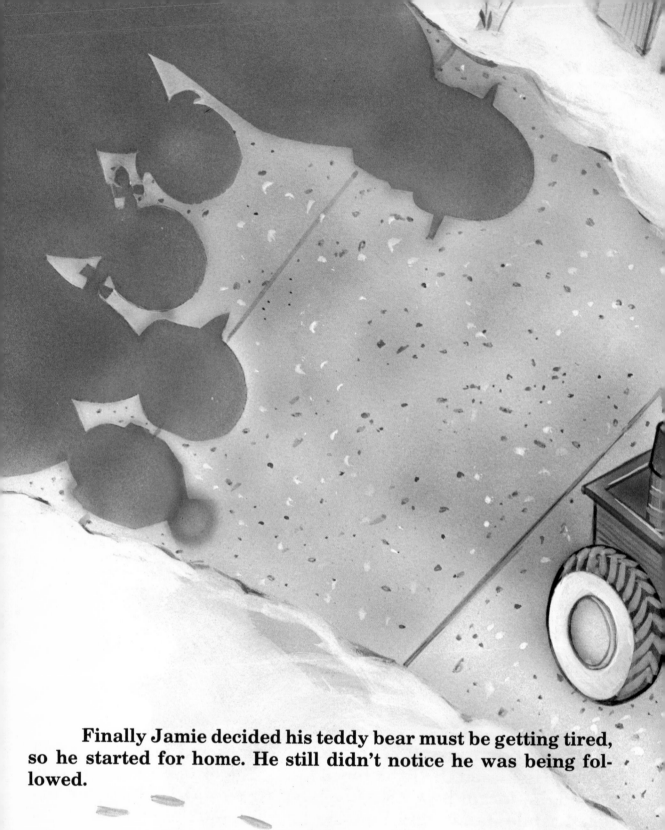

Finally Jamie decided his teddy bear must be getting tired, so he started for home. He still didn't notice he was being followed.

On the way home he saw a lady walking with a cane. Some big boys ran past her and knocked the cane out of her hand. She wasn't crippled, but she couldn't seem to find the cane. Jamie ran and picked it up for her. When he handed it to her, he understood why she couldn't find it. She was blind.

"I'm Jamie," he told her, "and I guess I can't see so good either. I can't seem to find the big, bright, beautiful star anywhere."

After he told the blind lady all about the star, he went on walking home. He didn't notice he was being followed as he walked through the gate to his house.

His father was waiting for him at the door.

"Did you find the star today, Jamie?" his father asked.

"No," said Jamie sadly.

"Well," asked his father, "who are these friends who came with you?"

Jamie turned to look.

There was the sad little girl, and the old man in the park. There was the little girl he had seen sitting on a stump, and the poor tired paper boy. There was the little boy on roller skates, and there was the blind lady.

"We saw it, Jamie!" they all said. "We saw the star!"

"Where? Oh, where?" cried Jamie. "Show it to me! I want to see it too!"

The sad little girl spoke first. "I saw it, Jamie, in the tear that glistened on your cheek when you felt sorry for me."

"And I saw it, Jamie," said the old man. "I saw it in your ears when you listened to me."

"I saw it in your voice when you were singing," said the little girl who had been sitting on a stump.

"I saw it in your hands when you gave me a drink of water," said the paper boy.

"When you kissed my knee," said the little boy on roller skates, "that's when I saw it. I saw the star by your mouth."

Then Jamie looked at the blind lady. Surely she couldn't have seen the star. But she spoke up.

"I saw it too, Jamie. I saw it brightest of all. I saw it in your heart."

And Jamie was very happy.

the story of Silent Night

By
JOHN TRAVERS MOORE

Illustrated

by

Bob Hyskell and Leonard Gray

Near blue Austrian mountains was a small church, and in it was an organ. It was not a new organ. It was quite an

old-fashioned one which went *pump-pump* each time it was played. But it was good enough for Father Josef Mohr, the kind priest of the church. When the church organist played it, it would wheeze and puff and creak its way through every song to God. And sometimes it even sounded very sure and strong.

There was no doubt that a new organ would have been much better. But Father Mohr had no hope of anything so grand as a new organ, for in the year 1818 money was scarce in Oberndorf, where the little church stood. Besides, this was in Austria with mountains nearby, and here even the wind makes a sort of music of its own, and singing is a part of life itself.

So it happened that on one starry evening no one was in the little church—that is, no one except church mice. The church waited, quiet and alone in the night, winter snows white and shining around it.

And in the quiet, a church mouse came out from his home in the wall because he was hungry.

Now, anyone knows that a church mouse is not rich. And when there are a number of church mice, the share is even smaller.

The first church mouse was soon joined by other church mice, who stole out beside him in the silence of the evening. Very softly into the night-world they came on tiny, velvet paws.

They looked this way—and that . . .

No one else was about.

All went noiselessly to the church organ. They peeked about once more—and crept in, each taking a wee bite of the leather of the organ bellows!

It didn't taste bad.

They tried it again.

It didn't taste good. But it didn't taste bad! It was a sort of in-between taste, made to fill a hungry stomach. And their stomachs were hungry.

"Have another bite?" one small gray mouse said to a second, who answered, "I believe I shall." Yet both were making themselves perfectly clear by doing instead of saying.

And since every gray mouse was busy in the same way, it was not long until one ate completely through the leather of the bellows. He found himself eating his way inside out, instead of outside in. And whichever way he went, he ate his way, as did the other mice: some ate in, and some out, until there were more holes than leather!

Suddenly there was a sound at the church door, then the squeak of a hinge. The door opened.

How they scurried, tumbling this way and every other way in their great hurry to hide! By the time Father Josef Mohr, the priest of the church, and the boy who pumped the organ bellows were inside, all was quiet.

Everything in the church was as still as the starry night outside.

"Thank you so much for coming with me this evening," Father Mohr told the boy. "I want to make sure all is ready for Christmas Eve services tomorrow night."

Father Mohr walked about the church, dim in the flickering lantern light. He shook his head as if satisfied, then said, "Let's try the organ now."

The village boy ran to the side of the organ, where he always pumped the bellows while the organist pressed the keys.

Father Mohr sat down at the organ. "Ready," he called.

The boy started to pump the bellows. But the bellows went *whoosh.*

My goodness!

Father Mohr pressed the keys. "Try it again," he said.

Once more the boy tried. *Whoosh* went the bellows. And the mice, who were listening, knew why.

They hung their heads.

"Christmas Eve—tomorrow night," Father Mohr said in a worried voice. "Something seems to be wrong with the bellows. If the bellows won't work, the organ won't play. What shall we do?"

"I have a guitar, Father," said the village boy. "I could play it."

"A very good suggestion," said the priest. "We shall call on you for the music."

They left the church, both feeling troubled. The boy was wondering how well he would play the guitar for the Christmas Eve services. And Father Mohr was wondering about Christmas Eve without carols played on his church organ.

Later that evening, Father Mohr sat in his study, thinking. Stars were bright outside his window. They filled him with a sense of peace, even with the problem he faced: Christmas Eve—in church—without an organ!

And there came to his mind the glory of the night about him. And it made him think of another night when a Babe was born in a manger. The thought came to him as softly as the fall of starlight. And since Father Mohr was a poet as well as a priest, he reached for paper and quill and put down words that told how he felt.

He read them over. It was a simple poem he had written, but one that would fit a plan.

"I shall go to Arnsdorf," he thought. "There, Franz Gruber may help me!"

He started at once from Oberndorf—where his little church was—to Arnsdorf, a village two miles away. And in some haste he plowed through the snows. On his way, he glanced up at the stars, feeling the nearness to heaven one feels on a starry night. The stars were silver-bright. Father Mohr looked ahead at the far lights of Arnsdorf: they themselves gleamed like fallen stars on the snow. He breathed deeply, moved on.

Through the cold he made his way in good time to the edge of the village of Arnsdorf. From there it was only a few steps to the schoolhouse where Franz Gruber taught. Franz was the schoolmaster of this neighboring village. But he was also Father Mohr's church organist. Father Mohr borrowed him from Arnsdorf for church services at Oberndorf every Sunday—no matter what the weather.

"Why, Father, what brings you here?" Franz said, when he saw the priest at the door. At first he thought something was wrong. But when he saw the twinkling eyes above the winter-nipped, pink cheeks and nose, he knew all was well. And so he added, "Come in, Father. Sit down! You bring good news?"

"You may find it interesting, Franz." The priest took off his greatcoat. "I have written a new poem, and I should like to have you hear it."

Father Mohr read the poem he had written.

And when he finished, he said, "Franz, I wonder if you could set this poem to music. It would be perfect for Christmas Eve services tomorrow night."

"I certainly can try, Father." Franz Gruber took the poem from the priest's hand. He read it silently. He was moved by the simple words and beautiful thoughts in the poem. They seemed to hold the beauty of the love which the Christ Child had brought upon the earth. "I'm sure it will make a good song, Father," said Franz. "Any poem this lovely deserves the best. I only hope my music will be suitable."

The two men shook hands. "I'll count on you, then," Father Mohr said merrily.

"Father—can't you stay and visit a little while?"

"No, Franz. The organ broke down, at last. I must go back and see that some practicing is done." Father explained that the village boy of Oberndorf was going to play the guitar for the Christmas services. "I thought he could play it while you sing the new carol," Father said.

"I don't have a wonderful singing voice, Father. But I shall be happy to try out your new carol, if you wish."

"I'll depend on you," the good priest smiled.

Through the frosted window, Franz Gruber watched Father Mohr make his way slowly back to Oberndorf across the shining snows. While Franz was gazing out the window, he, as Father Mohr had done, noticed the brightness of the stars.

He looked down at Father Mohr's poem in his hand. He read it over, then took it over to the lamplight and read it again. He memorized the first stanza.

Then, throwing a cloak around his shoulders, he went out into the night to look at the stars. In the clear skies above him, they shone in their lasting glory. Franz felt a strange longing inside of him—a longing to be among the stars, because they were so beautiful. He could almost feel the silence of the mountains ridged in the distance. But in the stars he sensed the very presence of a lasting light. They shone as they had through the ages. Only at the moment they appeared even more bright in the quiet of peace, where mountains waited patiently and valleys lay silver with fallen snow. It was truly a silent night, Franz Gruber thought, a holy night—even as tomorrow night was to be a very special one to celebrate the coming birthday of the King of love.

Franz began to hum. He could not help himself. It was as if his whole heart were singing a lovely, wonderful song of the stars.

Silent night, holy night

Inspired by Father Mohr's poem, Franz Gruber hummed again the simple melody that fit the words so well. The night about him remained peaceful and calm. A thousand stars looked down, their faces shining with the brightness of the children of God.

He hurried back into the schoolhouse. There he noted down the song, setting his music to the words of the poem. Tomorrow night there would be a new carol for the Christmas Eve program at Oberndorf!

Franz fell asleep that night with a feeling of great peace.

The next evening found him at the Oberndorf church, along with Father Mohr and the villagers.

A boy was there, too, with his guitar. He did not have a good guitar, but it was one with all six strings, ready to be played—most willingly.

And when the time came for the Christmas service to begin, all the people of Oberndorf glanced at Franz Gruber, waiting for him to go to the organ and play it. But he did not.

There followed the sound of only one man singing—Franz Gruber. He did not have a perfect voice, but it was passable. And only one boy played the guitar as Franz Gruber sang. Truthfully, he did not play it as well as an accomplished guitarist might. Yet he kept firmly within the bounds of a few safe chords.

And while the singing went on to the strumming of brave fingers on a battered guitar, Heaven knew of it. One may be sure. Certainly the angels listened, though no words were spoken from on high. Yet there is no doubt that the angels smiled a little, as they listened. It would be very difficult to imagine anyone who would not smile and feel the warmth of Christmas when hearing such a song—even as they first heard it . . .

Silent Night! Holy ...

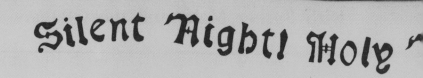

Si - lent night! Ho - ly night!

all is bright, Round yon Vir - gin M

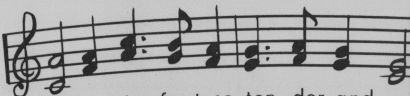

Ho - ly In - fant, so ten - der and mi

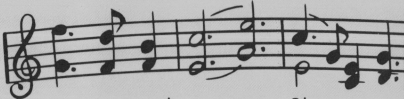

heav - en - ly peace, Sleep in hec

And so the notes drifted into silence, as softly as a prayer among the stars.

And that is how the people of Oberndorf, on that night of long ago, listened to the words and the music of a new song, hearing the words as they were first sung, and the music as it was first played.

Yet the church mice there had listened also.

They said nothing about why the organ was not played, for mice cannot talk. But mice can feel sorry—and hang their heads! And yet, the more those little church mice thought about what they had heard, the less sorry they felt. It was they, it must be remembered, who had made it possible for the world's greatest carol to be sung on the world's greatest night—the Eve of Christmas.